A Cane in Her Hand

By Ada B. Litchfield
Pictures by Eleanor Mill

Albert Whitman & Company, Morton Grove, Illinois

The author wishes to express appreciation to the following people whose guidance made the writing of this story possible:
Kenneth Stuckey, Research Librarian, Perkins School for the Blind, Watertown, Massachusetts;
Billie Louise Bentzen, Instructor, Division of Special Education and Rehabilitation, Boston College, Chestnut Hill, Massachusetts;
Elizabeth A. Peebles, Graduate Student, Education of the Visually Handicapped and Peripatology, Boston College.

Readers who seek information about children who are visually handicapped or blind may wish to write to
The American Foundation for the Blind, Inc., 15 West 16th Street, New York, New York 10011 or to
Perkins School for the Blind, 175 North Beacon Street, Watertown, Massachusetts 02172.

Library of Congress Cataloging-in-Publication Data

Litchfield, Ada Bassett.
    A cane in her hand.

    (A Concept book)
    SUMMARY: A young girl finds ways to cope with her failing vision.
    [1. Blind—Fiction]   I. Mill, Eleanor.   II. Title.
PZ7.L697Can   [Fic]   77-14255
ISBN 0-8075-1056-4

About Valerie's Story

Valerie is a visually impaired child. She is not totally blind, but even with the help of glasses, she does not see as other children do.

Children having low vision need help in coping with their poorly-seen world, and they need much understanding from their families, peers, and teachers. When the right help is given, these children become happy, well-adjusted participants in regular family, school, and community activities.

A child having a severe visual problem may see less clearly than other children, and the visual field may be imperfect. Low objects, for example, may not be seen unless the child looks down at them. The child's eyes may be uncomfortable, and the vision from time to time may vary greatly.

Special teachers can be of assistance. They teach study skills, daily living skills, and travel skills to visually impaired students. They help each girl or boy make the best use of remaining vision and of other senses. Children who have low vision are often helped by learning to use special materials: large print books, optical aids such as magnification systems, and travel aids such as a long cane.

Valerie's difficulties, frustrations, and accomplishments will have special meaning for children in similar circumstances. For others, Valerie's story is intended to create feelings of understanding and acceptance toward visually impaired persons. Such positive attitudes are necessary if those with visual problems are to lead full and happy lives.

BILLIE LOUISE BENTZEN
Division of Special Education and Rehabilitation
Boston College
Chestnut Hill, Massachusetts

My name is Valerie Sindoni, and I don't use my long cane all the time.

Sometimes I don't need it. I don't need it when I go to Roger's house. He's my cousin and lives next door. I've been to Roger's house so many times I know every step of the way there.

Why do I have a long cane? Because I can't see very well—that's why.

The thick glasses I wear always helped me. But one day I found that even with my glasses I wasn't seeing well. That was a no-good day.

I couldn't find my new jeans when I got up. I banged into the bathroom door and hurt my knee. I spilled my piggybank and lost some of my pennies and dimes. I couldn't see well enough to find all of them.

After breakfast, my sister Susan asked me to play with her. She was cutting out pictures. I really didn't want to.

"I can't cut out this dog, Sue," I said.

"Push your glasses up on your nose and try," she said. I tried. But Sue screamed, "Wait! You've cut off his tail."

"I don't see any tail," I said, squinting my eyes up and looking at Susan. I felt mad.

Squinting my eyes helped a little, but Susan looked like a big gray blob, not like Susan. But of course she didn't know that.

"Oh, you!" Susan said, taking the scissors away from me. "Stop squinting and go play with Roger."

"Okay, okay," I said. I grabbed my Frisbee and ran.

Outside, I saw something moving in Roger's yard. It was Roger with his little sister Ruthie behind him. They were coming out of a gray fog. That's strange, I thought.

I ran toward them. But I stubbed my toe and fell.

"Hey," Roger yelled. "Look where you're going. You blind or something?"

"I guess so," I said, pushing myself up and feeling around for my Frisbee and glasses.

"No fooling, Val?" Roger asked in a worried voice. "Didn't you see that rock? Maybe you need new glasses."

"Naw," I said. "I need to look where I'm going. Let's play!"

"Yeh," Roger said, clapping his hands together.

"Here it comes," I yelled, and sent the Frisbee sailing.

"Ow!" Ruthie cried. "You hit me."

"I didn't mean to," I mumbled.

Roger didn't get hit, but he made a fuss anyway. "Hey, look what you're doing. Here I am. You must be blind."

To tell the truth, I was having trouble seeing Roger. He kept disappearing in a fog. I knew it wasn't a foggy day.

Ruthie said, "Don't worry. I know you didn't mean it."

But I was worried. I had a sharp pain in my left eye. Like the fog, it came and went.

"I'm going home," I yelled at Roger.

"Why?" he called back.

"I can't see you," I yelled.

"Aw, cut it out," he shouted. "Of course you can." But I was already running and stumbling home.

"Hey, Val," Roger bellowed, chasing after me. "I didn't mean that about being blind. Come back and play."

"Forget it," I told him and ran into my house and slammed the door.

My mother was worried when I told her about the pain. She made me go to my room and lie down. "Try to nap," she said. "At least close your eyes. I think the pain will stop."

After she tucked me in bed I heard her go downstairs and call my father and the doctor.

I had a nap and the pain went away, but the fog didn't. When I woke up, the furniture in my room looked different. It seemed to jump in my way when I got up to go downstairs.

The next day was Sunday. My mother kept me in bed. I didn't have any more pain, but I wasn't seeing any better.

Monday I didn't go to school. Instead, I went with Mom and Dad to see Dr. King. He was glad to see me, and that made me feel better. He took me into a room where he'd tested my eyes before.

Dr. King asked me questions. Did my eyes sting? Were they watery? Did bright lights make them hurt?

I pointed to my left eye. "This one hurts," I said. "I just can't see through the fog."

After awhile, Dr. King put drops in my eyes. He had me sit in the waiting room with other people while he talked with my parents.

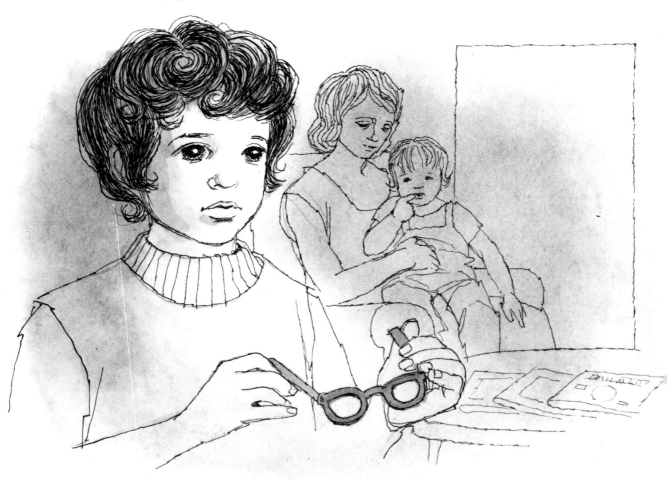

I could only see light and dark. I wondered if the other people had drops in their eyes, too.

Soon the nurse led me back to Dr. King. He spent some time flashing bright lights in my eyes. I didn't like that.

"I know this is no fun, Valerie," Dr. King said. "But it will be over in a minute. I have to find what's wrong."

"Am I going to have to go to the hospital, Dr. King?" I asked. I had an operation on my right eye when I was little. It didn't help much. I still couldn't see very well with that eye.

"I don't think so, Val," the doctor said. "But I will have to check your eyes every few days." I thought he sounded worried. That made me worried, too.

"Am I going to be blind, Dr. King?" I asked. I felt like crying.

"We hope not, Val," he said slowly. "We're going to do all we can to keep that from happening."

Soon Mom was holding my hand. She said, "Dr. King wants us to talk to your teacher, Val. She can help you at school."

"She already does," I said. "She lets me go right up to the chalkboard to see stuff. She gives me books with large print to read. And special paper with black lines and a special pencil, too. What else can Mrs. Johnson do?"

"We'll have to find out," my father said.

"Sorry about the eyedrops," Dr. King said when he told me goodbye. I still couldn't see much. But I said, "It's okay." He's nice. He wants to help me.

I had a cheeseburger with everything when we had lunch in a restaurant. But I was too upset to eat. I was thinking about the special room at school where kids go for extra help. I didn't want to go there. I'd miss the other kids and Mrs. Johnson too much.

When Dr. King said it was okay, I went back to school. Mom went with me. She talked to Mrs. Johnson and other people.

Nothing happened right away. But it was a bad time. Lessons are hard when you can't see well. And I kept bumping into things even when I tried my best to see what was in the way.

Then one Monday Mrs. Johnson told me, "Miss Sousa is here. She's the special teacher for children who have trouble seeing. She helps with lessons, and maybe she'll teach you how to travel by yourself so you won't get lost or hurt."

It sounded sort of all right, but I hated to go to another room and leave my friends, even for a little while.

After Mrs. Johnson went back to the other kids, Miss Sousa gave me a test.

She showed me some book pages. I read those I could see to her.

Then we talked about how people who can't see well get around. By listening carefully. Touching. Feeling with their hands and their whole bodies sometimes. Things I'd been doing for a long time without thinking about it.

I did okay, but I was glad to go back to my own room.

I saw Miss Sousa two days a week after that. She helped me with schoolwork. She showed me how to hold my hands and arms so I wouldn't run smack into things I didn't see. I liked Miss Sousa—she's so nice you can't help liking her. I began to think coming to her room wasn't too bad.

Then one day when I came in, Miss Sousa held something out to me. A long cane. Right away I began to worry.

"Oh, no!" I shouted. "I don't need that. Only blind people use canes. I'm not blind. I don't want it."

Miss Sousa didn't get mad. She said, "You know, Val, you're getting a lot of bumps lately. It's because you don't see some of the low things in your way. Your hands and arms don't reach far enough."

Well, that was true. It's no fun running into things. It hurts and it makes you feel stupid. I could use some help.

Miss Sousa put the cane in my hand. "A long cane is like a long arm," she said. "With it, you will find the low things before you bump into them. You won't be saying Ouch! so often."

"A long skinny arm," I said, and Miss Sousa laughed.

She went on, "I've moved chairs and things around in this room. I'm going to the other side of the room. I want you to follow me. Use your eyes and ears. Walk slowly. Use the cane as if it were your hand to find anything in your way."

I tried a few steps and moved the cane from side to side in front of me.

Ping! The cane hit the trash basket. I knew it was the trash basket by the sound it made. So I used the cane to find enough space to walk around it.

Plunk! A heavy chair. *Plink!* The leg of a metal table. I walked around everything.

"How about that!" Miss Sousa said, clapping her hands. "You followed me across the room and didn't bump into anything." I felt sort of proud. But I didn't like the noise the cane made and the way it felt clumsy in my hand. Still, it was fun to guess what things were from the sounds they made.

"Do you know what you were doing?" Miss Sousa asked. "You were cane traveling. It's not easy to be a good cane traveler. Let me show you how to use your cane so it won't be so noisy and clumsy."

I nodded my head, but I wasn't too happy about it.

In the next weeks Miss Sousa taught me how to hold and use a long cane to travel indoors. I was glad we practiced in her room. It was easier with just the two of us. Each time she put more things in my way. I learned to tell what was in my way by the sound it made and how it felt when I touched it with the cane. Then I found how to go around it.

"Val," Miss Sousa said one day, "you're becoming a very good cane traveler." She made it sound like being a good swimmer or skater. Then she said, "Let me know when you want to practice in the hall."

"Hmmm," I thought to myself. I didn't like the idea. In the room it was okay, but maybe people in the hall wouldn't understand. How about my friends?

Well! They understood. It didn't make any difference to them. Miss Sousa had me practice going from my room to the gym and to the music room. I had my own cane now. I used it inside those rooms, too. People always move stuff around, but I don't bump into anything when I use my cane.

Later, I took my cane outdoors and learned how to find the edge of the walk or a hedge or a fence to help me stay on the path. Miss Sousa stayed right with me.

After that, I took my cane home. The kids saw me and wanted to know how to use it. I showed them.

Everybody found a long stick and practiced walking.
Roger did better than anyone else. He would. The big
show-off.

Now my long cane takes lots of bumps for me. I use it at school, especially going to different rooms. I take it with me when I go places. I don't often go to new places alone. But someday I will, and my cane will keep me from bumping into things or falling when I come to a curb.

Once I used my long cane to poke Roger. He was being fresh as usual. He called me Pokey. So when he got close enough, I poked him. Hard. He yelled so loud that my mother came running. She was mad at me. Wow!

Mom was right. My long cane is not a toy. I'm not supposed to fool around with it.

Do I mind not being able to see as well as other kids? Yes, I do. But what I mind most is having people talk about me as if I'm not there.

One day I went to the store for Mom. Mrs. Wong, who owns the store, was talking to a lady whose voice I didn't know.

The lady saw my cane and said, "She's such a pretty little girl. Too bad she can't see."

That hurt! It made me mad, too. Didn't she think I could hear her? Or did she think I was too dumb to understand?

"I'm not deaf!" I screamed. I hurried out of the store and went home.

Mrs. Wong understood. It made her mad, too. She knows there are lots of things a kid can do without being able to see very well. She knows I can do most things kids in my neighborhood do.

I roller-skate. (So I fall down sometimes—so does everybody.) I swim. (At camp I won a medal for swimming.) I paint pictures and make things out of clay. I am learning to play the organ. I take dancing lessons. I make my own bed. I wash dishes, too—ugh!

I have learned to do many things. And like the other kids, I'm going to learn a lot more. Miss Sousa says the most important thing I'm learning is to think for myself.

I wish other people would learn that, too. Then they'd know there are lots of ways of seeing. Seeing with your eyes is important, but it isn't everything.